EDINBURGH FRIGHTS
CHILLING TALES
FROM THE CITY'S DARK PAST

Created and Written by
Scott Taylor

Illustrations by
Anastasia Cartovenco

THIS BOOK IS DEDICATED TO MY EDINBURGH FAMILY AND FRIENDS

EDINBURGH FRIGHTS
CHILLING TALES FROM THE CITY'S DARK PAST

ISBN: 979-8-218-48825-3

Copyright © 2025 Scott A Taylor. All rights reserved

No part of this book may be reproduced or utilised in any form or by any means, electronic or mechanical, including photocopying, recording or by any information storage and retrieval system without permission in writing.

SECOND EDITION

First Printing 2024. This Edition 2025
Concept, Words and Design by Scott Taylor
Additional icons: shutterstock.com
Edited by Nina Abbott

Original illustrations by Anastasia Cartovenco
Cover design by Scott Taylor, from original illustrations by Anastasia Cartovenco
satnaya.wixsite.com/karminaart

EDINBURGHFRIGHTS

EDINBURGH OLD TOWN

DEACON BRODIE

A respected member of Edinburgh society, William Brodie was a skillful cabinet maker, talented locksmith and serving as Deacon of the Incorporation of Wrights and Masons, a title that gave him a position of influence in the running of the city.

Through his work, however, Brodie was able to make copies of keys to wealthy establishments and homes around the city. In 1768, he and his gang of housebreakers started entering homes at night, stealing money, silver, and jewellery.

A CRIME SPREE OF 18 YEARS

It was a disastrous armed raid in 1786, that led to the gang's downfall. Two of his men were caught, but Brodie fled to Amsterdam to escape capture. He was quickly found, arrested and returned to Edinburgh to stand trial.

Deacon Brodie was hanged at the Tolbooth in October 1788.

In an ironic twist of fate, he was hanged on a new style of gallows that he himself had engineered!

THE MERCAT DEATH LIST

For hundreds of years, one of the major monuments of Edinburgh's history has been the Mercat Cross, a focal point for trade, proclamations and executions.

SCOTTISH SATAN

Turning up regularly in old stories invited or usually uninvited, is the Devil. Known by many names throughout the land such as Auld Clootie, The Earl o' Hell, Auld Nick and the demon Plotcock.

Around midnight in the month of July 1513, a demon appeared on the Mercat Cross, reading aloud a list of city Burgesses, Barons and Noblemen who would die in the upcoming battle of Flodden.

Upon hearing his name being read, Richard Lawson, the Lord Provost who lived nearby, threw a silver coin at the demon on the cross in order to appeal against his own upcoming death sentence.

GOOD OMENS

Richard Lawson became the only survivor that was on the demons list that day, with over 10,000 men losing their lives in one of the bloodiest battles in British History.

CANNONGATE CANNIBAL

10-year-old James Douglas was the 3rd Marquess of Queensberry with residence in the lower Cannongate. Considering his family's high standing in the city, very few people even knew he existed.

LOCKED OUT OF SIGHT

Considered violent and insane from an early age, James was kept under lock and key in a secret room on the ground floor of the house, away from other people, with only a few servants aware of his presence.

In 1707, the signing of the Act of Union, to bring the country together, had the city and Queensbury house in disarray as James' father was one of the main figures involved. With no one on duty that night, the young Earl had free reign of the house.

As James made his way to the kitchens, he found a servant boy working. From hunger or rage, he slaughtered the boy and roasted him in the large kitchen fireplace.

James Douglas had began eating him before he was discovered that night.

HALF HANGIT MAGGIE DICKSON

Margaret (Maggie) Dickson was born in Edinburgh but worked at an Inn as a housekeeper in the borders.

Maggie had a secret love affair, but her baby was born prematurely and died within a couple of hours. She couldn't afford to lose her job so she hid the body in a blanket at the river Tweed, so no one would know.

The body was soon found, however and Maggie was publicly hanged in the Grassmarket for child murder in 1724.

Maggie's body was placed in a coffin for her family, but on-route to her burial, she woke up screaming, dazed and confused.

Somehow, Maggie had survived her hanging.

EDINBURGH LAW

By law, Maggie had served her execution sentence and could not be hanged a second time.

She was well enough to walk all the way back into Edinburgh from Musselburgh that day and lived for several decades after that.

After Maggie's incident, the law changed and hanged until dead was added to the sentence.

Kirkyard is an old Scottish name for churchyard.

GREYFRIARS KIRKYARD

The Kirkyard was founded in Edinburgh, one year after Mary Queen of Scots returned to Scotland, opening in 1562. Its main purpose was to alleviate the overcrowded graveyard of St Giles Cathedral on the Royal Mile, and for centuries was the only graveyard in the most overcrowded area of any European city!

Below the graves that are visible in the Kirkyard today, is an even deeper level of the dead. At least 500,000 bodies were thrown into mass graves as space ran out in the other city graveyards. They were piled on top of each other and this is why Greyfriars is walled in at the Grassmarket and higher than the surrounding streets.

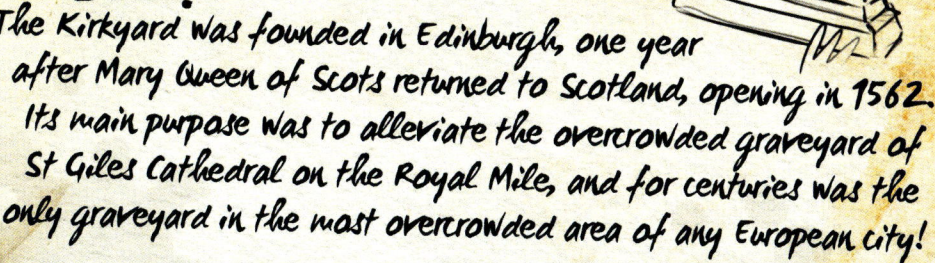

The topsoil is so thin that bones pop up every so often!

RESURRECTION MEN

As schools of anatomy expanded in Edinburgh, the need for corpses to dissect was in demand more than ever. So scarce were bodies that a thriving trade in exhuming bodies from the ground emerged. Resurrection men would dig up recently buried bodies during the night and sell them to doctors.

Wealthy families of the deceased started placing iron cages over the coffins of loved ones until their bodies were in a state no longer suitable for the doctor's dissection table.

EDINBURGH PLAGUE DOCTOR

In the year 1645, thousands of people died in the worst (and 10th) plague outbreak in Edinburgh's history.

A plague doctor visited contaminated properties on a daily basis and was dressed in a long thick leather cloak with a large brimmed hat and a crow-beaked mask that was filled with sweet-smelling herbs. Doctors believed the herbs would repel the 'evil smells' which were thought to carry the disease.

It was, however, fleas on the backs of rats that spread the disease like wildfire throughout the old town.

EDINBURGH'S SECOND PLAGUE DOCTOR

George Rae was appointed doctor in 1645 and promised a large salary for his work (and risk) treating the sick. The city authorities anticipated that Rae would die from being infected and had no intention of paying him.

For 10 years he battled to get what he was promised but died without receiving the money.

THE MACKENZIE POLTERGEIST PART I

On the south wall of Greyfriars stands the imposing mausoleum of Sir George Mackenzie, once Lord Advocate of Scotland.

He had a vicious reputation as one of the most evil persecutors of the Covenanters - the people who rose up to defend their faith in the Church of Scotland from Charles I.

One winter night, a homeless man in need of shelter broke into the mausoleum to keep warm. Thinking there were valuables in the caskets, he tried to crack one of them open, but the floor beneath him gave way and he fell into a dark chamber below.

He fell into the plague pits from years before, containing partially decomposed bodies and bones of Edinburgh's dead.

As he burst back through the entrance doors terrified, stories say he wasn't the only one to leave the mausoleum that night!

BLUIDY GEORGE MACKENZIE

George Mackenzie imprisoned over 1,200 Covenanters, torturing, starving and leaving them outside in the brutal Scottish weather. With ghostly attacks happening near his tomb, George Mackenzie seems to be as horrific in death as he was in life.

ANNIE'S ROOM

Under the busy cobbled road and thin closes of Edinburgh's Royal Mile, sits a vast labyrinth of streets and tunnels that were once the overcrowded heart of the old town, where rich and poor lived on top of each other.

MARY KING'S CLOSE

In a small cold room between two old closes, the presence of sadness is felt as a little girl called Annie is all alone and lost.

ALLAN'S CLOSE

SHE WANTS TO GO HOME AND SEE HER FAMILY

Annie's spirit has appeared next to the fireplace in a small corner of the room where she has communicated the loss of her parents and her favourite doll.

Over the years as Annie's ghost story has spread, people worldwide have left dolls and gifts for her to comfort and ease her spirit.

THE SECRET OF WRYCHTISHOUSIS

A mansion by the name of Wrychtishousis (Wright's Houses) was originally located on the corner of what is now Brunstfield Links.

Over the years, it passed through a series of owners, with Lieutenant General Archibald Robertson residing there on his return from the American War of Independence in 1783.

A servant to General Robertson stayed in a ground-floor room and each night was visited by a terrifying ghost.

NIGHTLY HAUNTINGS

The apparition appeared as a headless woman, carrying a baby in her arms, she would walk from one side of the room to the other every night, week after week. No one paid much attention to the servant's stories, just that the room had a very strange feeling.

A very strange feeling, for a very good reason!

Years later when the house was being demolished, a makeshift coffin in the foundations was discovered. It contained the remains of a woman, whose head had been removed to fit her body in the coffin and whose arms held an infant, both fully dressed. Hidden away, and forgotten about.

THE CASTLE DRUMMER BOY

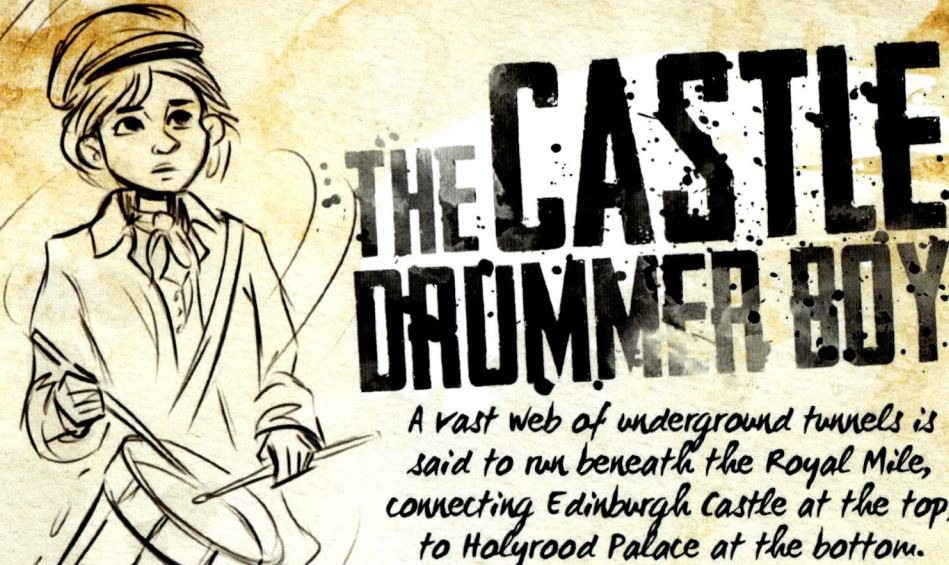

A vast web of underground tunnels is said to run beneath the Royal Mile, connecting Edinburgh Castle at the top, to Holyrood Palace at the bottom. Rumoured to be used in secret by royalty as an escape route when the castle was under attack.

THE DEPTHS OF THE CASTLE

Many years ago, the entrance to the underground tunnels were discovered in the castle depths, but no one knew for certain where they led to, so a young boy was sent down with a drum to squeeze through the dark passages and find out exactly where they led.

Beating his drum as he descended, he could be heard on the street above, the further he went, the further the tunnels seemed to go.

But at the Tron Kirk - halfway down the Royal Mile - his underground drumming stopped. Soldiers went down as far as they could to look for the boy, but he was never seen again.

If you walk down Castle Hill on a quiet night, you might hear the drums beating from the tunnels below your feet.

THE MACKENZIE POLTERGEIST PART 2

When George Mackenzie died in 1691, he was buried in Greyfriars, right next to the Covenanter's Prison where he had imprisoned and tortured so many people. It is believed this is the reason for his restless spirit, tormented in death, for his actions in life.

BEHIND LOCKED GATES

There have been hundreds of accounts of ghostly apparitions, poltergeist attacks and general strange phenomena surrounding the Covenanter's Prison, where people have sustained bruises, bites and scratches whilst visiting over the years.

Many people have been knocked to the ground and even rendered unconscious by the dark and malevolent spirits that linger behind the locked gates at the south wall of Greyfriars Kirkyard.

BLUIDY MACKENZIE, COME OUT IF YE DAUR
LIFT THE SNECK AND DRAW THE BAR!

For hundreds of years children have shouted this through the keyhole of the mausoleum doors at night, daring each other to awaken the restless spirit of George Mackenzie.

It seems something was indeed awakened!

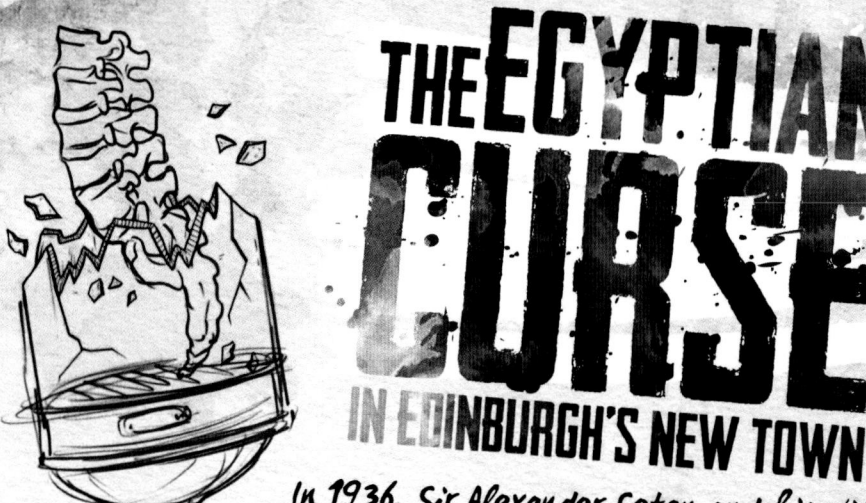

THE EGYPTIAN CURSE
IN EDINBURGH'S NEW TOWN

In 1936, Sir Alexander Seton and his wife Zeyla were on holiday in Egypt. During a day trip to a recently excavated dig site arranged by a local guide, Zeyla noticed a pit full of skeletal remains. She secretly picked up a section of lower spine bone and hid it in her bag as a souvenir from her adventure.

On returning to Edinburgh, the bone was put in a glass display case - that's when strange things started to happen!

DARK AND DANGEROUS FORCES

First, a huge area of their ceiling came crashing to the floor, then the sound of heavy footsteps on the stairs. An ancient ghostly figure standing in the shadows would be seen by guests and overnight rooms were ransacked with books, paintings and ornaments all destroyed, including one occasion when the glass case itself was smashed. This activity continued for months.

Over 80 people including researchers and collectors offered to take the cursed bone to a museum or return it to Egypt, but Sir Alexander ultimately had it exorcised and burned by a priest.

Howard Carter, the discoverer of King Tut's tomb sent a letter to the Setons, stating he was aware of paranormal activity happening around other Egyptian relics removed from tombs.

PRISONS AND PUNISHMENT

The main function of a prison in 17th Century Edinburgh was simply a place to keep prisoners until they could stand trial. If found guilty this could mean mutilation, banishment or public execution. In these times, there were over 200 offenses which carried the death penalty.

For over 400 years, the Old Tolbooth Prison occupied a site outside St Giles on the Royal Mile. There were iron collars fixed to the outside walls for chaining up offenders in public view and spikes above, to exhibit heads taken from executed prisoners.

Minor offenses such as begging could lead to being burned on the cheek by hot branding irons or having your ears nailed to wooden posts or even removed completely. Following any more crimes you would be banished from the country and risked being hanged if you returned.

BEGGAR'S BADGE

Edinburgh was so overrun with poverty, and beggars were in such large numbers that as a way to control the destitute, each was issued with a badge if they wished to continue begging legally.

This large metal badge was worn around the neck or fastened to a belt and had to be on display at all times to authorities.

Beggars were forced to stay in one small area, as their badges only allowed them to beg in the borough in which it was issued.

THE BLACK DINNER

In 1437, King James I of Scotland was murdered, making his 6-year-old son, James II, King of Scotland. Being so young, he was relocated to Edinburgh Castle for safety.

A THREAT TO THE KING

Clan Douglas was led by the headstrong 16-year-old William, 6th Earl of Douglas, who were enemies of the crown. Sir Alexander Livingston and Sir William Crichton, Keeper of Edinburgh and Stirling Castle were very aware of the power Clan Douglas had.

William and his younger brother David were invited to present themselves at court in Edinburgh Castle to have dinner with the young King James II, as an act of reconciliation between the clan and the crown.

The dinner was interrupted by the placing of a black bull's head on the table. Under old Scottish custom, this signaled death for any guests in the presence of the King.

The two Douglas boys were given a mock trial finding them guilty of treason and beheaded.

Following the death of the boys, their uncle James, known as 'James the Gross' became the 7th Earl of Douglas. It was said he turned a blind eye to knowledge of the murders, thus inheriting all the Douglas Estates.

WIZARD OF THE WEST BOW

Major Thomas Weir moved to Edinburgh in the early 1600s becoming commander of the town guard after a long military career. He was a well known and popular figure after his retirement, staying in the West Bow - a winding street that ran from the Royal Mile down towards the Grassmarket.

Upon his 70th birthday however, he shocked city residents by confessing to years of vile wickedness and satanic rituals.

A GIFT FROM THE DEVIL

He told Edinburgh authorities of the power of his walking cane, claiming it was the source of great power that had been given to him by the Devil himself. He would ride to the countryside in a carriage pulled by six fiery horses to practice all manner of demonic behaviour, sorcery and witchcraft.

He was immediately locked up in the Tolbooth Prison stating, "I have lived as a beast and I shall die as a beast" before he was hanged and burned (along with his cane) for his lurid crimes.

For over 100 years, no one in Edinburgh was brave enough to enter Thomas Weir's West Bow property, stating its nightmarish atmosphere from decades of use in unholy practices.

BURKE AND HARE

Edinburgh in the 19th century was the leading city for anatomical teaching, there was however, quite a shortage of bodies.

In 1827, William Hare was renting out his lodgings, when one of his guests suddenly died. Along with his friend William Burke, they decided to sell the body to Dr. Robert Knox, who was always in need of fresh bodies to dissect for his medical students.

Over a 10-month killing spree, 16 people from Edinburgh's Old Town were murdered and sold to Dr. Knox, who turned a blind eye and paid them well at around £10 a corpse.

They ultimately became too careless in their greed for money. Witnesses spotted them dumping a body outside the anatomy labs and alerted the city authorities.

EXECUTED 28 JANUARY 1829

Once they were caught, Hare testified against Burke, and walked free of any crimes — as did Dr. Knox, due to his high medical status in the city.

William Burke was hanged in Edinburgh's Lawnmarket and his body was publicly dissected by Dr. Alexander Monro at the University's Anatomy Theatre, where his skeleton still hangs on display today!

Around 25,000 people watched William Burke being hanged, paying up to 20 shillings (around £1) to get a good view.

THE GREAT LAFAYETTE

As a friend of Harry Houdini, the Great Lafayette (Sigmund Neuberger) was the highest-paid magician of his time!

Following successful vaudeville-style tours in the USA that included his dramatic illusions and disappearing acts, the Great Lafayette arrived in Edinburgh with over 40 performers and a menagerie of animals to perform at the Empire Theatre (Edinburgh Festival Theatre) in 1911.

Four days later, in a freak accident, a lantern set fire to the stage, killing 10 people including the Great Lafayette.

A TRUE MAGICIAN OF MYSTERY

The body of Lafayette was soon found and sent to Glasgow for cremation. Two days later however, an unusual discovery was made under the stage, another body, identically dressed as Lafayette!

His ghost haunts the theatre today, standing in the dark wings of the stage with the sounds of his beloved animals still echoing around the venue.

THE GHOST ROOM

There is a legend surrounding Bruntsfield House dating back over 200 years when Sir George Warrender owned the estate.

The house sits tall with its red brick facade and windows of various sizes, once covered in thick ivy. These windows were brought into question in 1820, with the discovery of more windows on the outside than inside, leading to the finding of a dark secret.

Hidden behind a tapestry in the wall was a narrow entrance to a hidden 'ghost' room that had been locked up long ago.

A LONG FORGOTTEN FIGHT

A dusty room was found just the way it had been left by a former occupant many years before. The fireplace still had ashes and the interior still had curtains that let in dim light.

Illuminated in the light were broken chairs, bottles and bloodstains on the floor showing signs of a fight. Crouched at the fireplace was the skeleton of an unknown man, stabbed by a now rusty sword, the loser in a long-forgotten feud.

MR BOOTS THE WATCHER

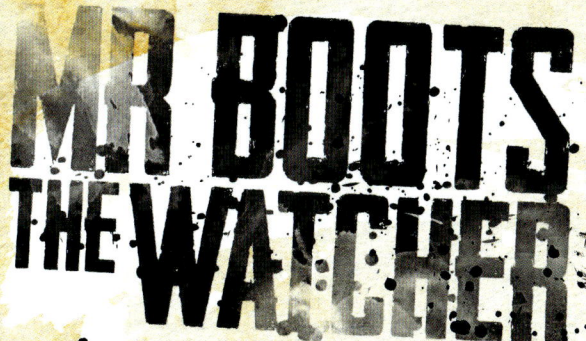

The Edinburgh Vaults are a series of chambers formed in the 19 arches of the South Bridge, opened in 1788, they were used for over 30 years as taverns, workshops, and storage space.

As the conditions in the vaults deteriorated due to dampness and poor air quality, the businesses all moved out, leaving a labyrinth of spaces, perfect for the city's worst villains and thieves to move in.

One resident of the vaults who has never left, is known as the Watcher. His menacing presence lurks in the dark recesses of the vaults, he is also known as 'Mr. Boots', named for his heavy boots that echo on the cobbles in the dark as he walks around keeping an eye on the rooms underground.

No one knows what his purpose was is in the vaults, all those years ago - was he a body snatcher or a murderer, or was he indeed a Watcher, patrolling the vaults? Sightings today have led to scratches on visitors and a strong stench of death in the air.

Living in, and visiting Edinburgh there is so much history on the doorstep, and always an excuse to go exploring.

Down cobbled streets and winding closes are true stories of gruesome events, terrible apparitions and many restless spirits that hide, just out of sight in every corner of this ancient city.

So go out and explore, who knows what you might see!

Along with various articles and online sources including:

The Warrender Letters 1715, Scottish Historical Society, folklorescotland.com, authenticvacations.com, mercattours.com thelittlehouseofhorrors.com eerieedinburgh.com, warfarehistorynetwork.com douglashistory.co.uk

Several books were also used as references in creating Edinburgh Frights:

Haunted Edinburgh by Alan Murdie, Horrible Histories Edinburgh by Terry Deary Ghostly Tales and Sinister Stories of Old Edinburgh by Alan J. Wilson, Des Brogan & Frank McGrail, The Ghost That Haunted Itself by Jan-Andrew Henderson, Edinburgh City of the Dead by Jan-Andrew Henderson, Crime Archive Burke & Hare by Alanna Knight, Supernatural Scotland by Eileen Dunlop, The Real Mary King's Close Guidebook.

 @ EDINBURGHFRIGHTS   @ SCOTTISHMYTHSANDMAGIC